Library of Congress Cataloging-in-Publication Data

Van Allsburg, Chris.
  The sweetest fig / written and illustrated by Chris van Allsburg.
    p.   cm.
  Summary: After being given two magical figs that make his dreams
come true, Monsieur Bibot sees his plans for future wealth upset by
his long-suffering dog.
    ISBN 0-395-67346-1
    [1. Dreams—Fiction.   2. Magic—Fiction.   3. Dogs—Fiction.]
I. Title.
PZ7.V266Sw   1993   93-12692
[Fic]—dc20   CIP
                        AC

Printed in the United States of America

HOR   10   9   8   7   6   5   4   3   2

The Sweetest Fig

CHRIS VAN ALLSBURG

Houghton Mifflin Company
Boston

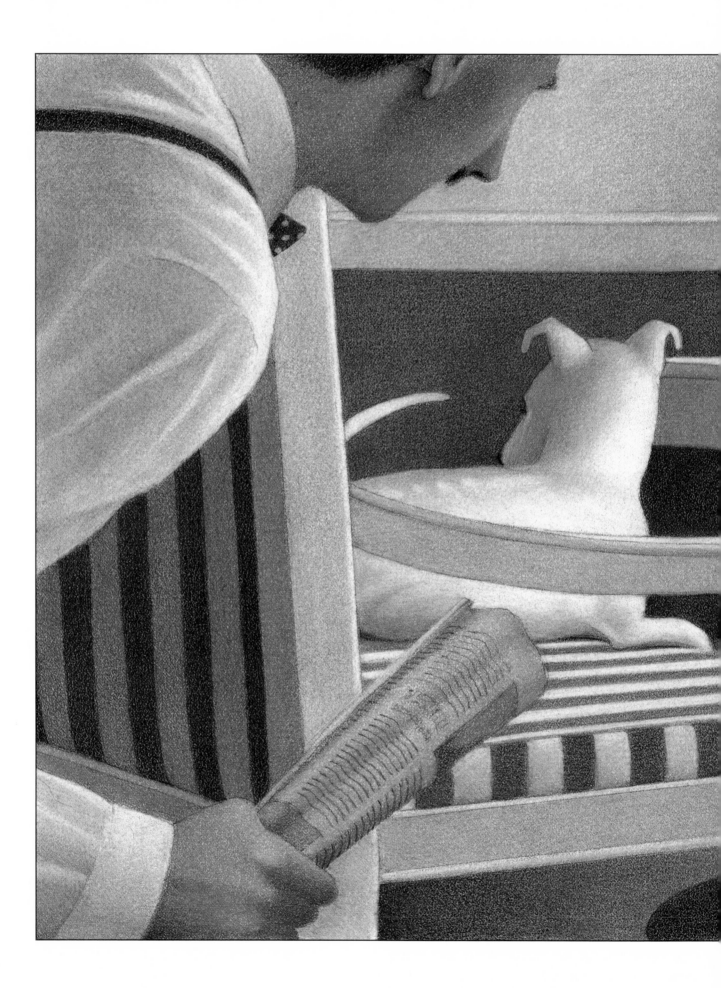

Monsieur Bibot, the dentist, was a very fussy man. He kept his small apartment as neat and clean as his office. If his dog, Marcel, jumped on the furniture, Bibot was sure to teach him a lesson. Except on Bastille Day, the poor animal was not even allowed to bark.

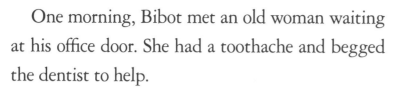

One morning, Bibot met an old woman waiting at his office door. She had a toothache and begged the dentist to help.

"But you have no appointment," he told her.

The woman moaned. Bibot looked at his watch. Perhaps there was time to make a few extra francs. He took her inside and looked in her mouth. "This tooth must come out," he said with a smile.

When he was done, the dentist said, "I will give you some pills to kill the pain."

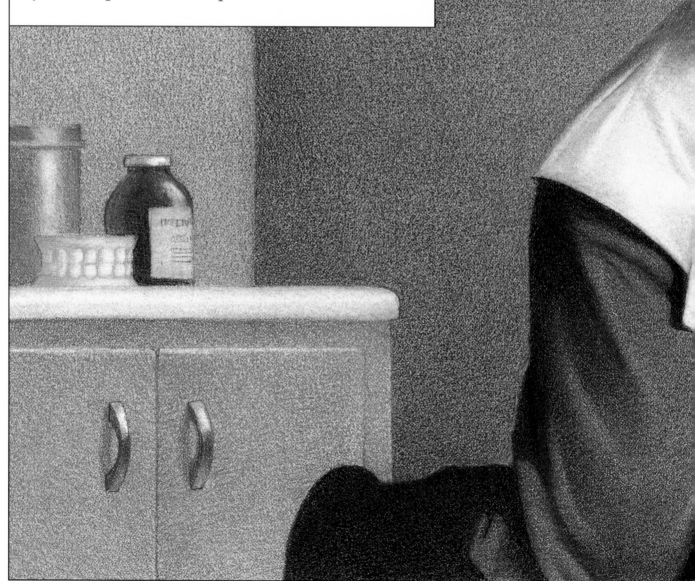

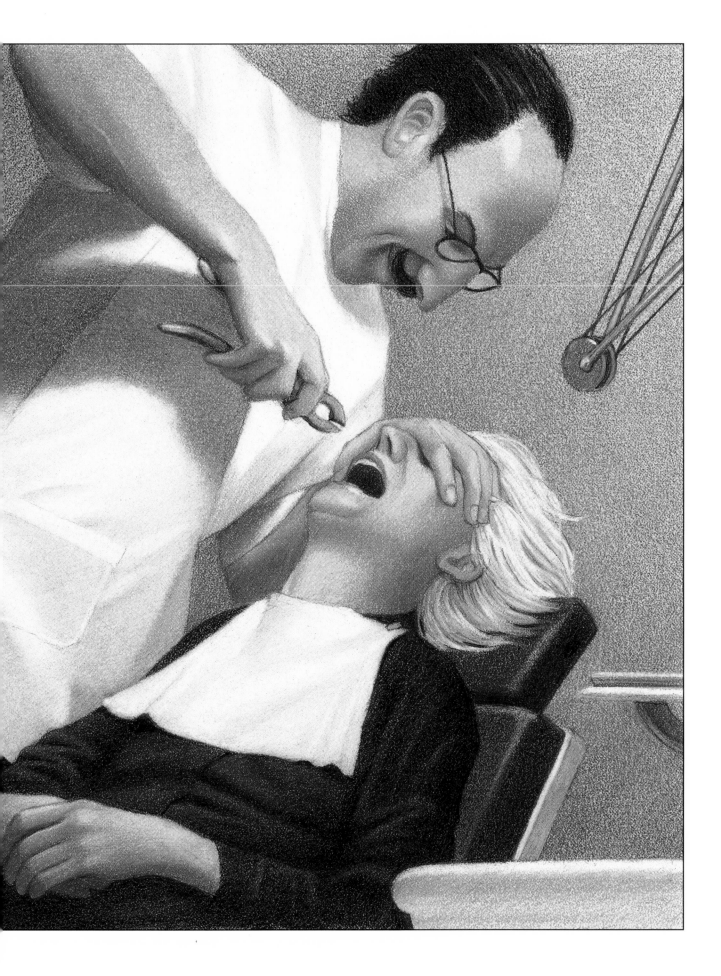

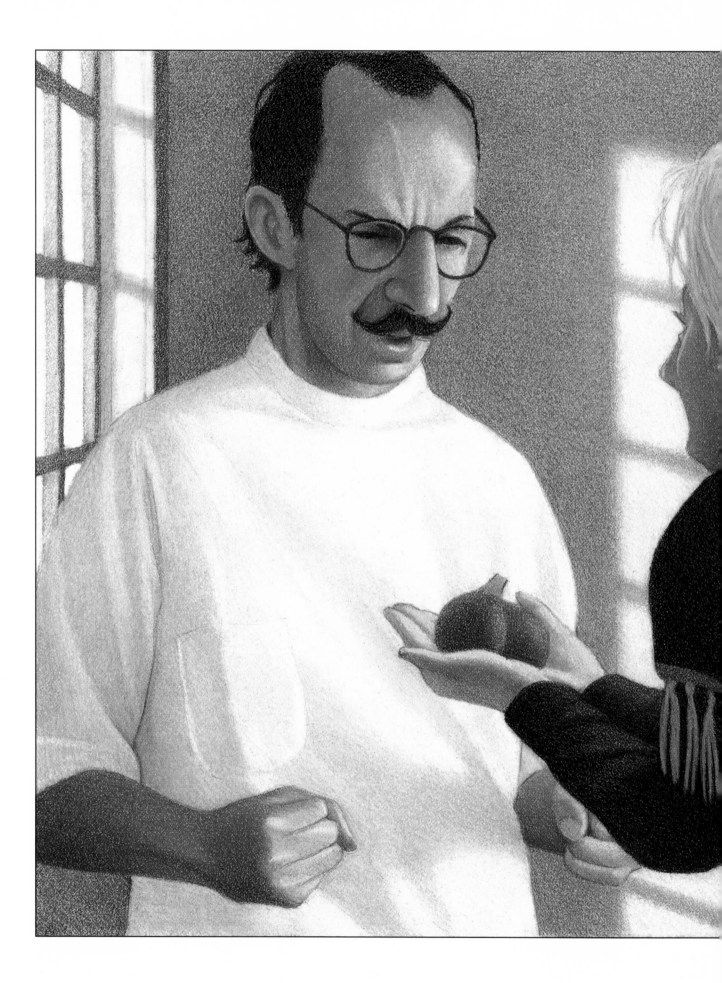

The old woman was very grateful. "I can't pay you in money, but I have something much better." She took two figs from her pocket and handed them to Bibot.

"Figs!?" he said angrily.

"These figs are very special," the woman whispered. "They can make your dreams come true." She winked at him and put her finger to her lips.

It was clear to Bibot that the woman was crazy. He set the figs down and took her by the arm. When she reminded him about the pills, he said, "I'm sorry, only for paying customers," and shoved her out the door.

That evening, Bibot took his little dog to the park. Poor Marcel loved to sniff the tree trunks and bushes, but whenever he stopped, Bibot would pull sharply on the leash.

Just before going to bed, the dentist had a small snack. He sat at his dining room table and ate one of the figs the old woman had given him. It was delicious. Possibly the finest, sweetest fig he'd ever had.

In the morning, Bibot dragged Marcel down the stairs for his morning walk. The steep steps were hard for the short-legged dog, but Bibot wouldn't think of carrying his pet. He hated to get Marcel's white hairs on his beautiful blue suit.

As he walked along the sidewalk, Bibot could not help noticing people looking at him. "They are admiring my suit," he thought. But when Bibot saw his reflection in the window of a café, he stopped in horror. He was dressed only in his underwear.

The dentist turned and ran into an alley. "Sacré bleu," he thought. "What has happened to my clothes?" Then he remembered the dream he'd had last night. In his dream, he'd stood in front of that very café, dressed in his underwear.

Something else had happened in his dream, and Bibot struggled to recall it. Marcel, looking out from the shadows of the alley, began to bark. The dentist looked up and saw the rest of his dream come true.

No one noticed Bibot as he ran home in his
underwear. All the eyes of Paris were fixed on
the Eiffel Tower, which slowly drooped over as
if it were made of soft rubber.

Bibot understood now that the old woman
with the figs had told him the truth. He would
not waste the second fig.

Over the next few weeks, as reconstruction of the Eiffel Tower began, the dentist read dozens of books on hypnotism. Each night before he went to sleep, he gazed into a mirror and whispered over and over, "Bibot is the richest man on earth, Bibot is the richest man on earth."

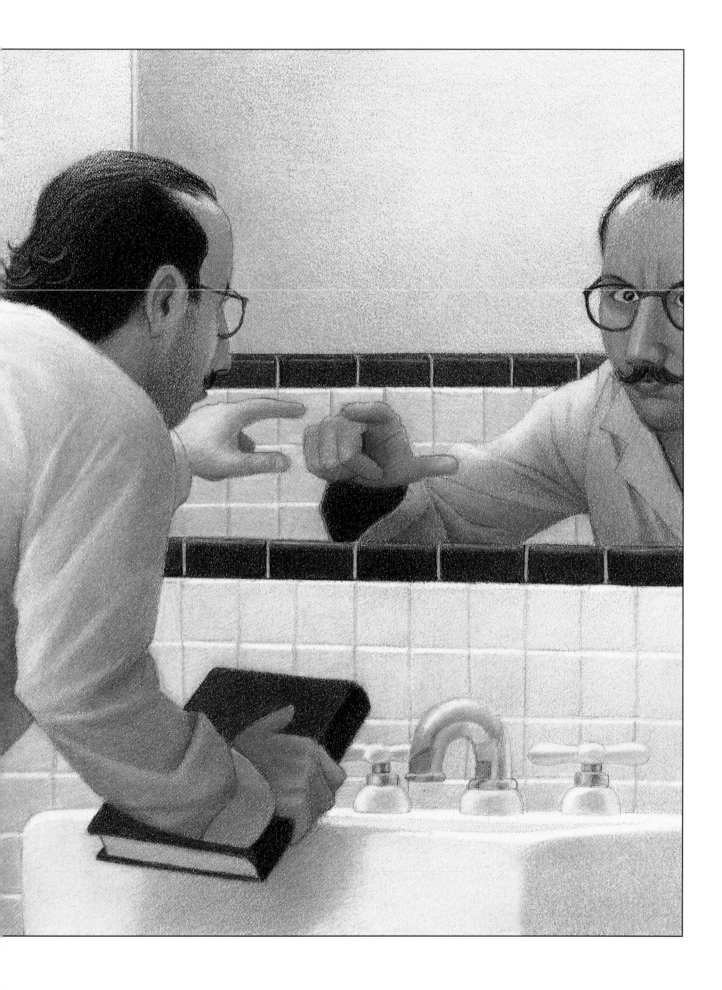

Soon, in his dreams, that's exactly what he was. As he slept, the dentist saw himself steering his speedboat, flying his aeroplane, and living in luxury on the Riviera. Night after night it was the same.

One evening, Bibot took the second fig from his cupboard. It would not last forever. "Tonight," he thought, "is the night." He put the ripe fruit on a dish and set it on his table. Tomorrow he would wake up the richest man in the world. He looked down at Marcel and smiled. The little dog would not be coming along. In his dreams Bibot had Great Danes.

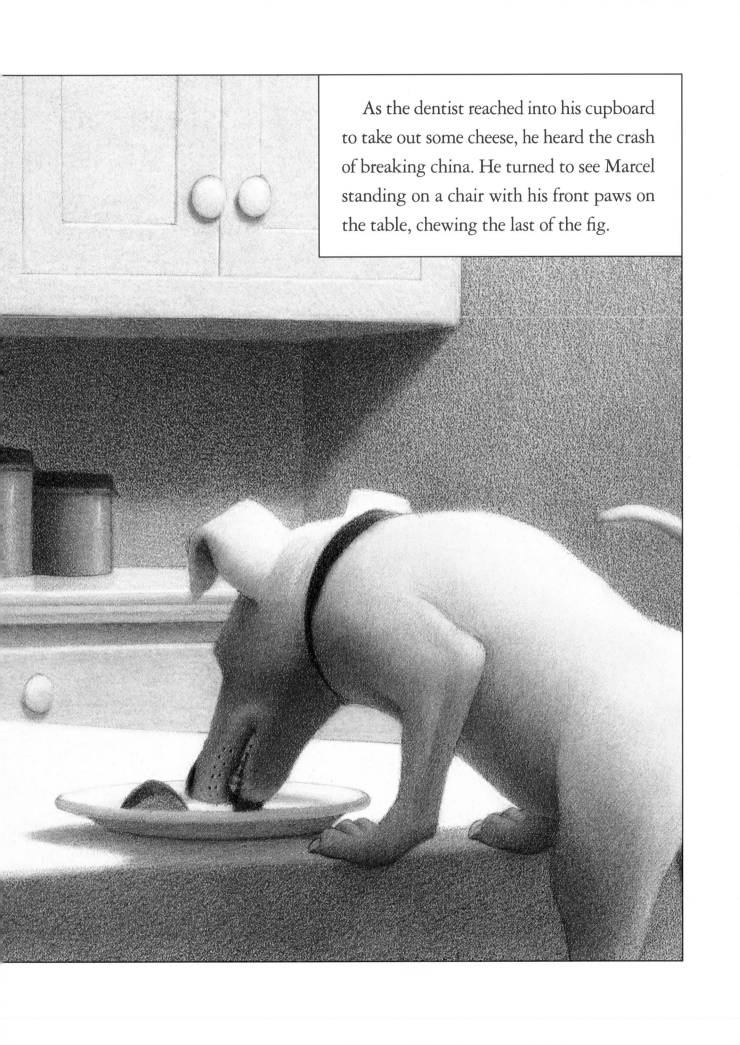

As the dentist reached into his cupboard to take out some cheese, he heard the crash of breaking china. He turned to see Marcel standing on a chair with his front paws on the table, chewing the last of the fig.

Bibot was furious! He chased the dog around the apartment. When Marcel ran beneath the bed Bibot yelled at him, "Tomorrow, I'll teach you a lesson you'll never forget!" Then the dentist, angry and heartbroken, went to sleep.

When he woke up the next morning, Bibot was confused. He was not in his bed. He was beneath it. Suddenly a face appeared in front of him — his own face!

"Time for your walk," it said. "Come to Marcel." A hand reached down and grabbed him. Bibot tried to yell, but all he could do was bark.

Dedicated To My Parents, Bee and Ed Wainwright;
My Sisters, Susan and Nancy and Their Wonderful Families.
Richard M. Wainwright

Dedicated To My Husband John.
Carolyn Sansone Dvorsack

FAMILY LIFE
PUBLISHING

Published by Family Life Publishing
Dennis, Massachusetts 02638

Printed in Singapore by Tien Wah Press
Published in the United States of America 1992

Library of Congress Cataloging in Publication Data

Wainwright, Richard M.
A New Life For Sir Christopher / written by Richard M. Wainwright:
illustrated by Carolyn Sansone Dvorsack,— 1st ed.
p. cm.
Summary: The adventures of a special wooden doll as he brings
love and happiness to children on two continents.
ISBN 0-9619566-4-X
[1. Dolls—Fiction 2. Wood Carving—Fiction.] I. Dvorsack Sansone, Carolyn,
1965 ill. II. Title
PZ7.W131Ne 1992 [fic]—dc20
91-26704 CIP AC

A New Life For
Sir
Christopher

Written by Richard M. Wainwright
Illustrated by Carolyn Sansone Dvorsack

To _____

Whatever you decide to be,

be the best you can.

Best Wishes,

Richard M. Wainwright

From _____

1

"Is it ever hot," Sir Christopher thought. "If only Sally would take off my busbee. Beaches certainly are not places for bearskin hats.

"Our first trip to Cape Cod; it really is beautiful. Soft white sand, gentle waves and fluffy white clouds floating across a dark blue sky are prettier than I ever imagined." Sally returned with her mother from swimming. Her father was lying on the blanket propped up on one elbow reading a mystery novel. Next to him was a cooler full of food and a large picnic basket that carried the suntan lotion, towels and books. Sir Christopher had been carefully positioned on top of the towels facing the ocean so he could see what was going on along the beach.

"Has Sir Christopher been behaving himself?" Sally asked her father. Sally's father looked up and smiled. "As always, Sir Christopher has been the perfect soldier, alert and watchful. But he looks very uncomfortable in his bearskin hat."

"Yes," Sally agreed, " I'm sure Sir Christopher would feel better without it." Sally knelt down next to the basket and gently removed Sir Christopher's busbee.

"Oh, that's so much better," Sir Christopher thought. "I wonder if Sally will take me for a swim. I've never been in the water and it looks like fun."

Sally and her mother opened up the cooler. "Time to eat and then take a nap," her mother announced. Sir Christopher watched contentedly as his family ate their picnic lunch. Afterwards they all lay down on their blankets to take a nap. Now Sir Christopher could relax. Before he let his thoughts wander he took one more look down the beach. A few parents and children were playing near the water. Others splashed in the gentle surf. All was well. The tide was slowly coming in.

Sir Christopher tried to think back as far as possible. He had only a vague feeling about his growing years somewhere deep in an Indonesian rain forest. He had been a small part of a huge satin tree that was cut into large blocks and shipped all over the world. He had arrived in Great Britain five years ago. It was really there his life began.

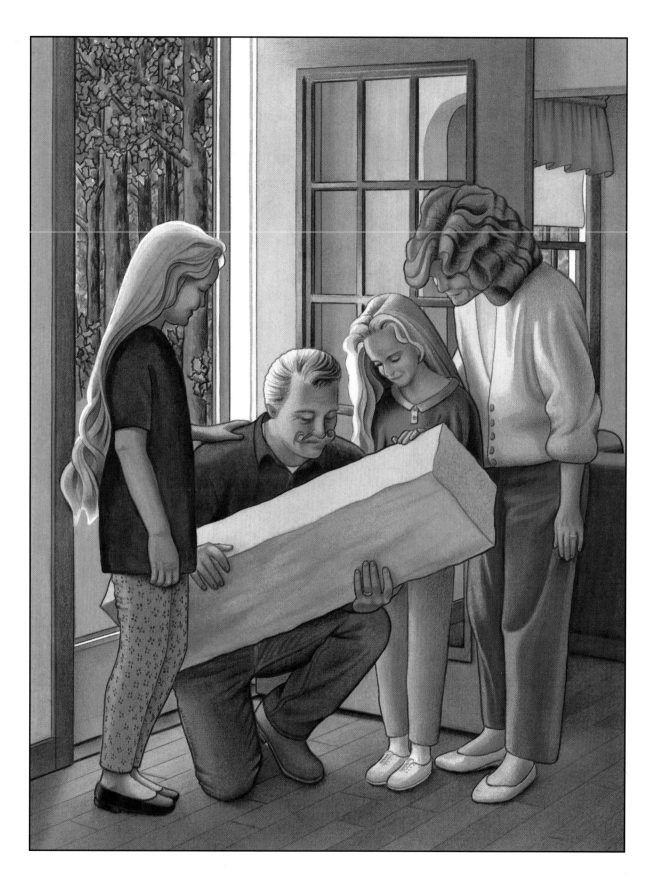

Although he was only part of a block of wood then, he could remember quite well a man with a strange accent coming into the lumber yard and asking the manager to show him the finest wood available. The two men stood above him. One reached down and lovingly touched the block of wood and then picked it up. Money was exchanged. Later Sir Christopher learned he had been bought with the meager savings of one Stanislaus Kozacko — newly arrived immigrant from Poland — master wood-carver and doll-maker.

Stanislaus loved to create dolls from beautiful wood, but since moving to London with his wife and two young children he had been barely able to earn enough money to buy food and pay for their four small rooms in an old part of the city. As he returned home with the wonderful piece of satin wood, he felt guilty knowing that he had spent a good portion of the family's savings. What if the children got sick and needed a doctor? What would he say to his good wife?

Stanislaus was determined to work even harder. When he arrived home, his wife Stefania wrapped her arms around him, which was not easy as Stanislaus was a very big man. And then he knelt to hug his two children, Kasia and Marlinka, who happily kissed him on each side of his large handlebar mustache.

"Papa, what are you going to do with that big piece of wood?" Kasia, the oldest daughter, asked.

"Someday, Kasia, when I have time, I will carve beautiful dolls from this piece of wood."

But Stanislaus did not have time for carving. Each morning he would get up before dawn and search for work. Some weeks he would help unload trucks, sometimes he washed dishes in a restaurant, and sometimes he spent his whole day unsuccessfully looking for work. By the time he arrived home at night it was often dark. Yet, when he came through the door, even when he felt sad and discouraged because he had not found work, he wore a big smile and laughed as he hugged his family.

One Saturday morning Stanislaus left early, as usual. Walking down a new street he saw a well-dressed man with his hands on his hips staring at a sad, old house. Stanislaus could see the basic structure of the house was solid and the architectural design pleasing, but the weary porch sagged, the broken windows pleaded to be fixed, and the sides of the house begged for a new coat of paint. As an experienced carpenter, he guessed the inside needed a great deal of work, too.

"Good morning, Sir." Stanislaus greeted the gentleman.

"Good morning to you, Sir," he replied. "But it would be a better morning for me if I could find a skilled carpenter to fix up this old house I bought yesterday. I know it needs a lot of work, but it is a lovely old house."

"I quite agree," said Stanislaus, "and if I may be so bold to say so, it is a lucky day for you and me. My name is Stanislaus Kozacko, and in Poland I was considered to be the best carpenter in Krakow. If you give me a chance you will not be sorry."

The gentleman smiled. "My friend," he said, "the job is yours and if you are dependable and as skilled as you say, there will be more work for you when you are finished."

For the first time since he had brought his family to England, Stanislaus had steady work and a steady income. How wonderful it was to look forward to Sundays, which now could be set aside for church, long walks in the city, or maybe even a picnic in the country. In the evenings Stanislaus' daughters would sit by his knees and read stories they brought home from school. After he and his wife tucked the girls in bed, Stanislaus took out his carving tools and sharpened them. Now he had time to think about making dolls again. He wanted his first doll in his new homeland to be very special.

On the second Sunday after he had begun working on the old house, Stanislaus decided it was time for the family to visit the famous historical sites of the city. His family had seen only the rather poor section they lived in because Stanislaus had begun looking for work the day they arrived in London.

After church, dressed in their Sunday best, with map in hand, Stanislaus proudly led his family first to the Tower of London, Parliament and Big Ben, and then announced to his family: "On to Buckingham Palace."

They followed the iron gate toward the main entrance of the Palace. There, standing on either side of the gate were members of the Queen's Guards who stood at attention. Stanislaus had never seen such men or uniforms. Each tall soldier wore a beautiful red jacket trimmed in gold, creased black pants and shiny shoes. On top of their heads were fur hats that added at least another foot to their height. The soldiers did not even blink their eyes as Stanislaus and his family moved closer. Stanislaus smiled and said to himself, "Gentlemen, in your honor, the first doll I carve in my new country will be a member of the Queen's Guards."

Immediately after work on Monday, Stanislaus took a bus to the city's library. He asked the librarian if there was a book on the Queen's Guards. She smiled and nodded. Ten minutes later Stanislaus headed home with several thick books under his arm. After dinner, Stanislaus settled in the old stuffed chair and began to read one of the books. His daughters looked over his shoulder and helped him with many of the words he didn't know. Their English had improved rapidly because they went to school every day.

The family sat like stones fascinated by the words Stanislaus was reading. The Grenadier Guards, the oldest regiment of the Foot Guards, was formed by Charles II in 1656. Their beautiful bearskin hats were made to commemorate a famous battle.

The second oldest of the regiments of Foot Guards were the Queen's Coldstream Guards. They, too, had a distinguished history, having courageously fought at Waterloo and later in World Wars I and II in Maylaya.

It took many nights for the family to finish reading all the books, but Stanislaus was determined to know everything possible about the Queen's Guards before he began carving the first doll. As he closed the last book he looked at his family and smiled. "Now I can begin. The first member of the Queen's Guards I will carve will be Sir Christopher James Ross, the hero of Waterloo. What do you all think?"

Everyone chorused their agreement. "And, Mother," Stanislaus continued, "do you think you and the girls could make Sir Christopher's uniform and bearskin hat?"

"Of course, Stanislaus," Stefania replied. "We would love to help. We'll begin looking for a bear right now, won't we girls?" Everyone laughed for a long time. But Stanislaus knew his wife and daughters were very clever and would create an exact replica of a Queen's Guards' soldier's uniform.

The following night after supper Stanislaus laid out his carving tools on the kitchen table. There were shiny steel knives, several types of chisels, gouges, and some wood-carver's rasps. Finally all was ready and he went to the closet to take out the large piece of satin wood he had bought many months ago. His first task would be to divide the block of wood into pieces. After measuring and marking the block with a pencil, he slowly cut the wood with a saw.

Two hours later he had eight blocks of wood, each twenty inches high and six inches square. Seven blocks were carried back to the closet. Stanislaus was ready. Taking up the pencil again, he carefully drew the outline of Sir Christopher and then picked up a small, very sharp chisel.

At first, large chips flew from the block of wood, but as the figure took shape Stanislaus began to work slower and slower. He could clearly see Sir Christopher imprisoned in the block of wood — it was simply a case of gradually setting him free and this would take time.

Night after night, Stanislaus would sit at the kitchen table with a small carving knife. Sometimes by midnight there would be only a tiny pile of wood chips even though he had been working for hours. Sir Christopher's body slowly emerged. Some nights Stanislaus would spend the whole evening carefully carving one of Sir Christopher's upper arms, forearms, and his hand and fingers. Later, his arms and legs would be attached to Sir Christopher's torso. Carving was exacting and tiring work. Occasionally Stanislaus would pause to rest and re-read about Sir Christopher and the Queen's Guards. Two months flew by but finally Stanislaus was satisfied. He knew that the following night he would attach Sir Christopher's arms and legs and insert Sir Christopher's blue glass eyes and then paint his face.

Back in the closet for the night, the wooden doll wondered what tomorrow would bring. He knew the life history of Sir Christopher, because Stanislaus often talked to him as he worked.

It wasn't that Stanislaus believed that a block of wood could hear, it was just that the family felt as the doll emerged from the wood, it was slowly coming to life. Tomorrow the doll would be Sir Christopher, and with glass eyes Sir Christopher would be able to see Stanislaus's face with its big mustache; the mustache his daughters loved to gently tug. He would see all the faces of his family, and so much more. "If dolls are born," he thought, "tomorrow will be my birthday."

The girls and Stanislaus's wife whispered in the living room. The night before, they had given Stanislaus Sir Christopher's colorful Queens Guards' uniform which they had cut and sewn by hand. Stanislaus had been very pleased when he saw their beautiful work. The girls knew their father would call them when he was finished. Although it was past their bedtime, Kasia and Marlinka were always allowed to stay up on these special nights.

"We're ready," Stanislaus called. Mother and daughters quickly walked into the kitchen.

Stanislaus was sitting at the table with the doll on his knee. In a deep, half-serious voice but with a twinkle in his eye, he spoke. "Ladies, I have the honor of presenting Sir Christopher James Ross, known simply to his friends as Sir Christopher."

Stanislaus' wife and daughters smiled and curtsied before rushing to take a close look at Sir Christopher. "He's handsome! Regal! Just wonderful! We love him Papa!" the girls exclaimed. From behind her back, Stanislaus' wife took a small box and handed it to her husband. He slowly opened it. Wrapped in tissue paper was a beautiful, doll-sized Queen's Guards' bearskin hat, complete with chin strap.

"Papa, I think we should take Sir Christopher to Buckingham Palace and show him to the Queen's Guards," Marlinka suggested.

"A capital idea!" replied Stanislaus, in his best imitation of an English accent. Everyone laughed. "Wear your best dresses. I want Sir Christopher to be proud of you."

It was just before noon on Sunday when Stanislaus and his family arrived at Buckingham Palace. Stanislaus was carrying a handsome wooden box that he had made for Sir Christopher. The two sentinels stared straight ahead, hardly moving. As Stanislaus took Sir Christopher out of the box and held him up for the Queen's Guards to see, a big black car stopped in front of the gate.

"Look, Daddy, what a beautiful soldier doll that man is holding!" cried a little girl who was looking out of the car window. "It looks just like one of the Queen's Guards. Can we get out to see it better?"

The little girl's father stopped the car and with his wife and daughter began to walk toward Stanislaus. Stanislaus and his family did not notice their approach, as they were laughing. One of the Queen's Guards had definitely winked and then smiled when Stanislaus held up Sir Christopher for him to see.

"Excuse us," the gentleman from the car said to Stanislaus. "I am the ambassador from the United States and we are on our way to say good-by to the Queen because we are returning to our country. My daughter saw your beautiful doll and wanted to see it better. My name is Allyn Woodward and this is my wife Lois, and my daughter, Sally."

Stanislaus smiled and shook the outstretched hand of the ambassador before introducing his wife and daughters. "Here, Sally," he said. "You may hold Sir Christopher, if you like." Sally beamed and cradled Sir Christopher in her arms. Stanislaus explained to the Ambassador and his family how he had made the doll and why they called him Sir Christopher.

"He is truly magnificent," the Ambassador exclaimed. "I have never seen a doll like it in England. I know the Queen would love to see Sir Christopher, too. Would you and your family come with us to meet the Queen?" For a moment Stanislaus was not sure he had heard correctly, but from the excited looks on his wife's and daughters' faces, he realized he had.

"That would be wonderful," he replied.

Stanislaus and his family followed the ambassador through the gates. Sally carried Sir Christopher, and Kasia and Marlinka walked beside her telling Sally Sir Christopher's life story. Inside the palace, they all waited in a richly decorated room for a few minutes before the Queen entered. The ladies and girls curtsied and the men bowed as the Queen approached and greeted the Ambassador and his family warmly. Stanislaus and his family were immediately introduced by the Ambassador, and Sally presented Sir Christopher to the Queen. The Queen was delighted to hold Sir Christopher and sat him on her lap. "You are a very talented man, Mr. Kozacko. Tell me about yourself and your family."

Stanislaus told the Queen about his life and work in Poland as a carpenter and master doll-maker, and his family's life in their new country.

The Queen spoke again as she handed Sir Christopher back to Sally. "I would love to have such a beautiful doll, and I know there are many other members of the Royal Family who would also like to buy one. Could you make more?"

Stanislaus could hardly speak. "It would be an honor. It is work I truly love. Thank you."

As the two families left the Palace, the Ambassador quietly asked Stanislaus if he would consider selling Sir Christopher. Everyone saw how much Sally loved the doll. Stanislaus spoke quietly with his daughters. "Of course, Papa," Kasia, the oldest daughter said. "Malinka agrees. We are happy to know that Sir Christopher will have a good home and be loved. We know you will make us another doll."

Sally, of course, was thrilled. The ambassador was delighted and gave Stanislaus three times the amount of money Stanislaus had suggested. "Mr. Kozacko," he said, "your talent is remarkable. People will be happy to pay this amount for your dolls. It is a very fair price. Open a shop and above the door place a sign: DOLL-MAKER OF THE QUEEN! You will be very successful, and some day you will be very famous. It was a pleasure meeting you and your lovely family, and be assured Sally will take good care of Sir Christopher."

After handshakes and hugs the two families said good-bye. The ambassador's words proved to be correct. After Stanislaus had made several dolls for the Queen, he opened a shop and had so many orders that making dolls again became his full-time work. He moved his family to a country home and as the ambassador predicted, became famous throughout England as the Master Doll-Maker of the Queen.

Sir Christopher thought back to that amazing first week of his life. In less than seven days he had seen the family who had created him, had been shown to the Queen's Guards, met the Queen of England, and become the dearly loved doll of the daughter of the former U.S. Ambassador to Great Britain. And that wasn't all. Sir Christopher had had his first ride in an airplane.

Sally held him up as they approached New York City so he could see where he was going to live. Although Sally told him it was near "Central Park," all Sir Christopher could see below him were the thousands of houses and office buildings. It was all so exciting.

The Ambassador had a lovely home in the city and Sally had her own beautiful room. When not in Sally's arms, Sir Christopher was placed on top of the bureau allowing him to watch over the room and also see out the window.

Sally took him everywhere. He had been to the Bronx Zoo, Central Park, Times Square, and even the Empire State Building. And now, here he was on Cape Cod.

His family continued to sleep soundly. Sir Christopher felt a gentle breeze which had climbed the dunes behind him and rushed out to sea. In only a few minutes the breeze became stronger and began to rattle and shake the beach umbrella. Sir Christopher was worried because dark clouds tumbling high above him quickly blocked out the sun. A large raindrop plopped on the beach umbrella, followed almost immediately by many more. Sally's father awoke first and saw a bad storm was just about on top of them. He woke his wife and daughter.

"We have no time to lose," he said as he took down the umbrella. "This storm came up behind us and it looks powerful. Quickly help me pack everything." Sally and her mother began tossing the towels, sun lotion, books and games into the basket, completely covering Sir Christopher. The rain came down in buckets and then a bolt of lightning hit nearby. The crackle and earsplitting boom of the thunder and lightning around them frightened Sally, and she began to cry.

"Time to run for the car!" her father shouted as he put the beach umbrella on his shoulder and scooped up the heavy basket with his other hand. Sally's mother carried the cooler and held tightly to Sally's hand. Crash — boom — another lightning bolt hit nearby. The wind whipped the beach umbrella in front of Sally's father's eyes and for a second he couldn't see where he was running. He tripped over a large rock. Sally's father flew through the air. The beach umbrella went in one direction and the basket somersaulted in another. Everything in the basket fell out and scattered all over the beach.

"Go on," he called to his wife and daughter who had stopped. "I'm all right and will be right behind you." The rain came down so hard it was like a gray curtain making it almost impossible for Sally's father to see. He hurriedly picked up the books, towels, games and bottle of sun lotion. He thought he had everything.

He didn't know Sir Christopher had been in the basket covered with towels. Once again, he picked up the basket and beach umbrella and began to run toward the dunes and the parking lot. Sally and her mother were already in the car. It took only a few moments for her father to open the car's trunk and put away the umbrella and basket. The family was wet and cold but they were safe.

Sir Christopher was wet too. He had landed in the sand behind a large boulder. His beautiful bearskin hat was nowhere to be seen. Facing the sea, through the mist of the heavy rain, Sir Christopher could see that the waves were not far away, and as each minute went by they came closer.

Sir Christopher was sad. He wondered if he would ever see Sally or her family again. The pounding surf crept toward him. It wasn't long before the first fingers of the incoming tide began to swirl and lick his shiny black boots. Minutes later, Sir Christopher was engulfed and seized by an advancing wave and swept toward the surf as the tide retreated toward the ocean. Up and over, around and down he went as a wave tossed him about, slowly carrying him out to sea.

Sir Christopher couldn't see anything except the white froth of the waves near the surface and the gritty swirl of sand when he was bounced off the bottom. He wondered if it would ever end. It seemed like forever before he popped to the surface and floated on his back. As the wind and tide carried him to the top of a large wave, he could see that the beach was now far, far away. Sir Christopher wondered what the ocean would do to him. "I am a soldier," he thought, "I must have the courage to accept whatever happens."

The storm raged on, carrying Sir Christopher further out to sea. His last glimpse of land was the tall Provincetown Monument on the tip of Cape Cod. All through the night the wind blew fiercely, pushing Sir Christopher further and further northward. By noon the following day the seas began to subside, the wind dropped, and a welcome sun played hide and seek with fast moving gray clouds. Sir Christopher felt a bump and then slid down the back of a large sea turtle that just happened to have surfaced under him. He watched it disappear marveling at how smoothly its flippers propelled it along. "I wonder what other things I will see."

Almost before he finished the thought, a school of playful dolphins appeared and one even jumped directly over Sir Christopher. They swam so fast that they were quickly out of sight. When all was quiet around him, Sir Christopher watched the sea gulls flying above him making lazy circles, endlessly searching for something good to eat. On clear nights, Sir Christopher wished upon the first twinkling star he saw, just as Sally always did. He hoped she and her family were all right and that her father had gotten her another doll to love. Days and nights passed with sun and more rain.

Sir Christopher floated for two weeks. His once beautiful uniform faded from the constant sun and his gold buttons were tarnished and pitted from the sea.

One morning, just as the sun was climbing over the horizon, Sir Christopher was shot up into the air as a playful baby whale exhaled, blowing vapor through the hole in her head. Kerplunck! Sir Christopher landed on the whale's back and for ten minutes enjoyed a ride on this magnificent creature. Sir Christopher thought, "If only this wonderful animal would take me back to the beach." But ten minutes later the whale sounded, and Sir Christopher was again floating alone in the ocean.

Waves gently rocked Sir Christopher back and forth. It was actually very pleasant. Now he knew why people enjoyed swimming. On he drifted.

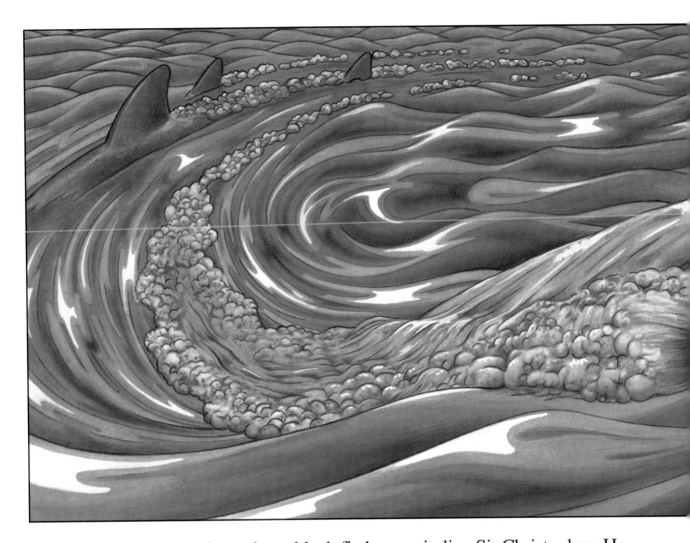

Later in the morning, a large black fin began circling Sir Christopher. He knew it was a fish but it didn't act like the other fish that had swum beside him, or the dolphins who always raced by. He watched the fin turn and face him and then swiftly cut through the water toward him. A few feet away a huge mouth with rows of razor sharp teeth opened. Sir Christopher was about to become breakfast for a hungry shark. A small wave tossed Sir Christopher to the right as the shark's jaws snapped shut, catching Sir Christopher's lower right leg. Crunch! The shark was gone and so was part of Sir Christopher's leg.

"Well," thought Sir Christopher, "I guess I was lucky, even though I lost part of a leg. I could be riding around in that shark's stomach and that isn't a very appealing idea."

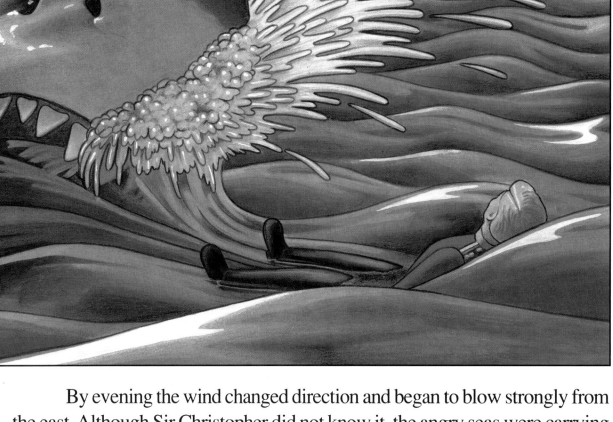

By evening the wind changed direction and began to blow strongly from the east. Although Sir Christopher did not know it, the angry seas were carrying him toward land. By sunrise, Sir Christopher heard the crashing of the waves on a very rocky shore. The coast of Maine was only a few hundred yards away.

As the waves pushed Sir Christopher closer to shore, the sounds of the pounding surf on the jagged rocks grew louder and louder. Sir Christopher was no longer recognizable as a member of the Queen's Guards. There was little color in his uniform and the sun had faded his golden hair to light gray. The rosy color of his cheeks was also gone. Only his shining blue eyes remained the same. He was now barely fifty yards from shore and he could see the huge rocks that shattered each advancing wave into millions of tiny drops of white water.

The battle between the rocks and waves soon engulfed Sir Christopher. Caught by the fingers of a large wave, he was hurled straight into the granite face of a black boulder. Sir Christopher slammed into the rock, tearing his jacket. A tiny chip from his back broke off and disappeared as the wave carried it away. Another wave picked him up as it attacked the shore only to be destroyed by a different granite sentinel. This time Sir Christopher's shoulder hit the rock a glancing blow. Back and forth floated Sir Christopher in the endless battle. By nightfall, what had been left of his uniform was now in shreds. He knew it would not be long before he would be broken into many pieces and his life as Sir Christopher would be no more.

Many miles away a gigantic wave formed and was now rushing toward the land. Sir Christopher, battered and dented, waited courageously for the next wave to hurl him against the wall of boulders. Almost gently the monster wave grasped Sir Christopher as it flew toward the shore. It towered above the rocks and rolled over them determined not to be stopped before reaching its goal — a narrow beach. Beyond the rocky barrier the wave finally broke on the soft white sand, depositing a thankful Sir Christopher before it returned to the sea.

Sir Christopher landed in a sitting position next to a large rock. He was a terrible sight. Almost nothing remained of his beautiful uniform. He was dented and had lost a few chips of wood, and thanks to the shark, part of his right leg was missing. But, even with all this, his eyes were still bright and one could see that he had once been a beautiful doll. Sir Christopher felt something squeezing his good leg. Looking down, he saw that a small crab was trying to determine if he was edible. It quickly decided Sir Christopher wasn't, and scurried away.

Sir Christopher could see a long way down the beach. A few seagulls patrolled the shore looking for clams or muscles to eat. Except for the birds it was a lonely beach. There were no houses nearby, yet above the high tide mark he could see one set of footprints. "There is always hope," he thought. "Maybe someone will come along."

The rain stopped, the wind slackened and the storm clouds drifted away. Sir Christopher spent the night looking at a starry sky, wondering what the future would bring. Maybe another storm would take him back to sea.

A crisp and bright dawn chased away the night. Sandpipers that had been dashing in and out of the surf looking for food suddenly took flight. The soft crunch of footsteps came closer and closer. A tanned and rough weathered hand reached down and picked up Sir Christopher, slowly turning him around to look at his face.

"Well, my friend, you have had a rough voyage," observed the old man. "I'm Toby Chace and I have lived in these parts for better than seventy years, and you're the first doll ever to visit my beach." Slowly examining Sir Christopher, the wrinkled face with twinkling eyes smiled and spoke again. "By golly, with some help from me, my little friend, you may be just what Matthew needs. Wait till Emma sees you — 'tis a lucky day for us."

It was a lucky day for Sir Christopher, too. He had no way of knowing that the old, retired sailor carrying him rapidly down the beach loved to fill his hours carving and painting beautiful seabirds. Toby Chace had sailed all over the world but now in his seventies, he sailed no more. His days were spent with his good wife and his daughter's family that lived nearby. Matthew, his youngest grandson, used to come by to listen to his grandfather tell tales of the sea and also tell his grandad about his life at school. Since the terrible accident, Matthew hadn't left his home and he didn't want to return to school at the end of the summer vacation.

Toby's home had been built on a bluff overlooking a lovely cove. He entered the side door and took Sir Christopher into the kitchen. Emma was shopping but she would be back soon. After spreading a blanket over the table he took out his carving tools and a small block of bass wood. Slowly he began to clean and sand Sir Christopher. When that was done, he picked up the small piece of wood and began to carve it. Occasionally he would stop and measure Sir Christopher's half leg, and sand it until it was smooth. By the end of an hour, Toby had made a fine peg leg for Sir Christopher, and it fit perfectly.

Examining the doll, Toby said, "Yes, I think you're ready for new clothes and a new life." With that, Toby put his sandpaper and knives away and returned to the table with acrylic paints and brushes.

"Joshua will be your name, my little friend," Toby said. "Tis a proud name of an ancient warrior and around these parts the equally famous name of a great sailor — Captain Joshua Nickerson."

Sir Christopher — now Captain Joshua — was as happy as a doll could be. His many days at sea and the storms which had nearly destroyed him had also almost destroyed his hope of ever being loved by a child again. Toby's tender loving care had restored this hope, and he wondered how he could possibly help Toby's grandson Matthew.

After a moment's rest, Toby began to paint Joshua's face — a face that had been aged by the sun, wind, and sea. Below his graying black hair, Toby gave Captain Joshua healthy, tanned cheeks. Then he painted Joshua's one boot shiny black, and finally he varnished Joshua's new peg leg.

"You're a handsome devil, Joshua, if I do say so myself," Toby chuckled. Just then Emma came through the door.

"Handsome, he is," Emma repeated. "Where did you get this beautiful doll?" Emma sat down next to Toby and listened. Toby told her of finding Joshua on the beach and his hope that Joshua might help Matthew.

After hearing Toby's story, Emma smiled and nodded. "I hope you are right," she whispered, "And now, the only thing your Captain Joshua needs is some good clothes — I think a white turtleneck sweater, a blue captain's jacket with brass buttons, and dark pants would be perfect. I can make them for him this evening. And tomorrow, let's take Captain Joshua to Matthew."

Immediately after breakfast the next morning, Emma and Toby went to Matthew's house. Matthew's mother and father greeted and hugged them. They were very discouraged because Matthew continued to stay in his room day after day. No matter what they said, Matthew hardly spoke and showed no interest in leaving his room. Toby carried Captain Joshua in a large paper bag under his arm. "I think it is time for this old man to have a talk with his grandson," Toby said. Leaving Emma to explain, he turned and began to climb the stairs to Matthew's room.

Matthew was sitting on his bed staring at the metal braces strapped to his right leg from the knee down. The doctors had told him he might always need them. He would never run like before. Matthew loved sports and had been the fastest boy on the baseball team. He knew he would never play baseball again and hardly looked up as his grandfather sat down next to him.

"Matthew, I would like you to meet a friend of mine," Toby began, as he took the doll out of the bag. "This is Captain Joshua Nickerson who lived in this village over one hundred years ago. Like you, he was born with two good legs and went to sea as a cabin boy on a schooner when he was only thirteen. On his second voyage to Europe, a terrible Atlantic storm tossed his ship about until two of the masts broke. Joshua was on deck at the time trying to help the sailors reef the sails but it was too late. With an ear splitting crack, Joshua looked up just as the masts began to fall. He tried to run but slipped on the watery deck and one of the masts fell on his right leg. It was crushed badly. The ship's doctor tried but could not save the boy's leg and Joshua returned home walking with the aid of crutches.

"For a little while he was very discouraged, but Joshua had courage. He loved the sea and had planned to make it his life. He decided a peg leg would not stop him. Joshua returned to school and studied everything that would make him a valuable sailor. He learned to read and write in order to keep the ship's log, and studied mathematics so he would be able to keep financial records.

"From an old sea captain he learned the science of navigation so he could sail a ship to any corner of the world.

"At age eighteen, he returned to the sea and adventure. He sailed to far away ports and learned several languages and was able to trade with people in distant lands. Once his ship was attacked by Caribbean pirates. Joshua's leadership and courage inspired his outnumbered sailors, and the pirates were soundly defeated. By age thirty, he became a captain of a fast clipper ship and as the years went by, Captain Joshua earned the reputation of being one of the finest men to ever sail the seven seas.

"Matthew, if you listen, I'm sure Captain Joshua would tell you about his adventures. I'll leave you two alone so you can get to know each other."

Matthew raised his eyes as his grandfather left his room and then stared at Captain Joshua. For the first time in many weeks a hint of a smile appeared on his face.

Emma and Matthew's parents wanted to know what had happened. Had Captain Joshua helped? Matthew's grandfather quietly replied that he had simply introduced Captain Joshua to Matthew and now they were getting to know each other. "I think we will know tomorrow," he said.

The next morning, Matthew's grandfather walked to the edge of the bluff overlooking the cove. He seemed to be waiting for something. "Emma! Emma!" he finally called. "Come out and see this wonderful sight." His wife rushed to his side and began to smile and then softly cry. Below them a familiar young boy in a rowboat was heading their way. As he rowed he appeared to be talking to a large doll that sat proudly in the stern of the boat. Born Sir Christopher, Captain Joshua's new life had begun.

*The
End*

They ran through a tunnel.

They chased little orange.

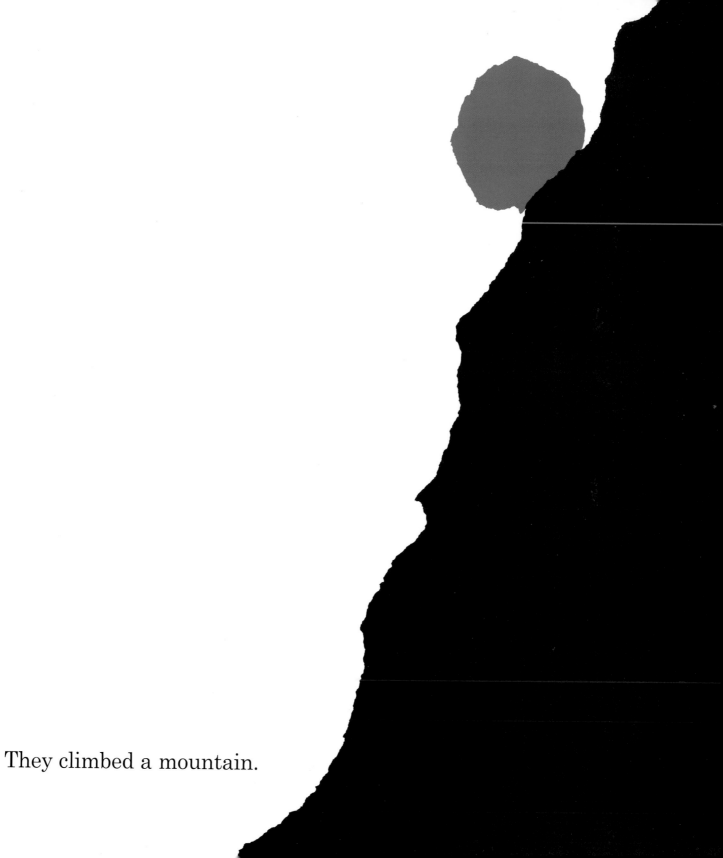

They climbed a mountain.

When they were tired

they went home.

But papa and mama blue said: "You are not our little blue—you are green."

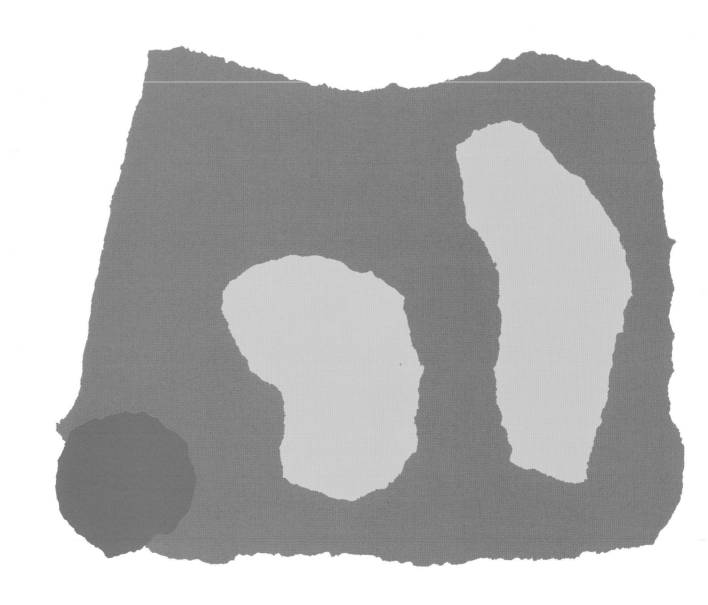

And papa and mama yellow said: "You are not our little yellow–you are green."

Little blue and little yellow were very sad. They cried big blue and yellow tears

They cried and cried until they were *all* tears.

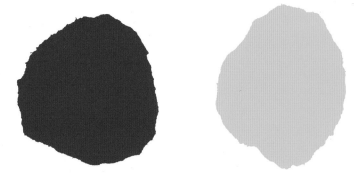

When they finally pulled themselves together they said: "Will they believe us now?"

Mama blue and papa blue were very happy to see their little blue.

They hugged and kissed him

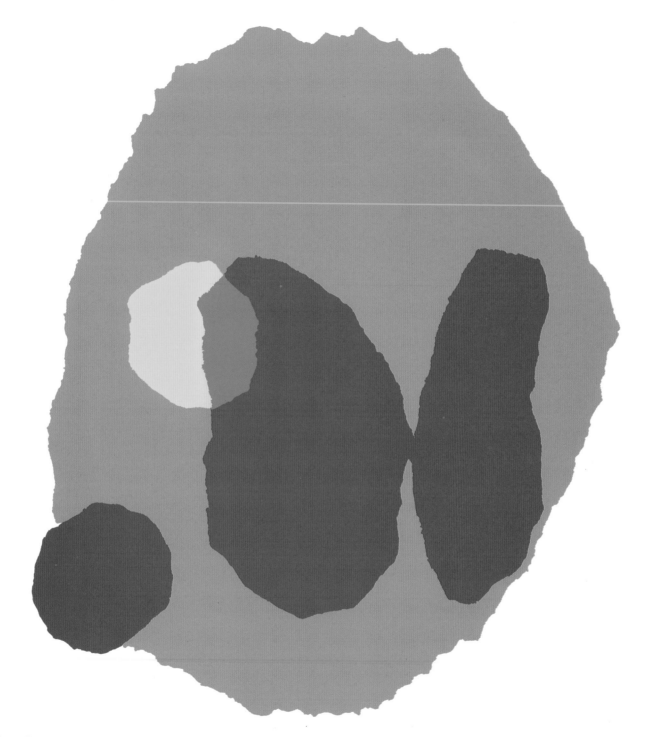

And they hugged little yellow too...but look...they became green!

Now they knew what had happened

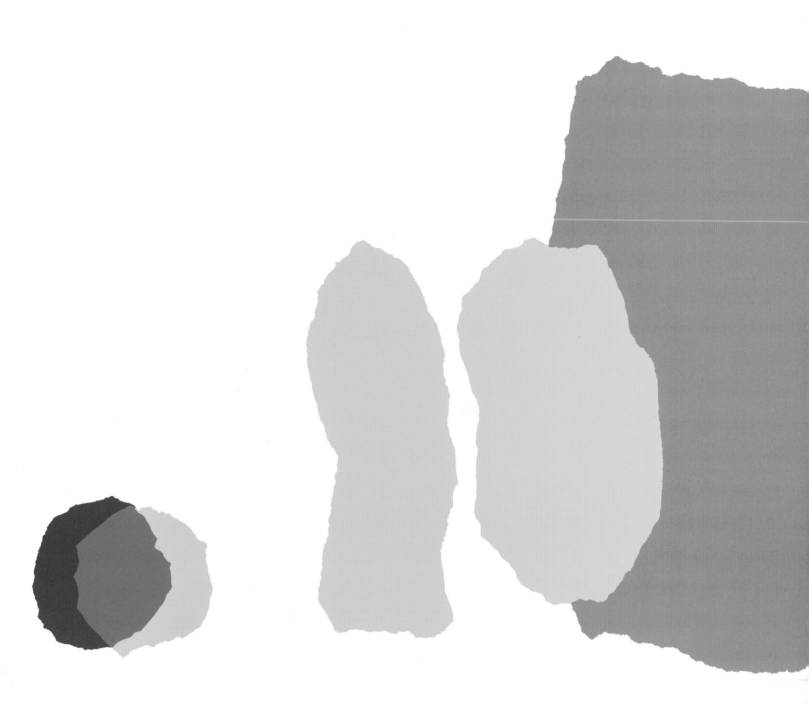

and so they went across the street to bring the good news.

They all hugged each other with joy

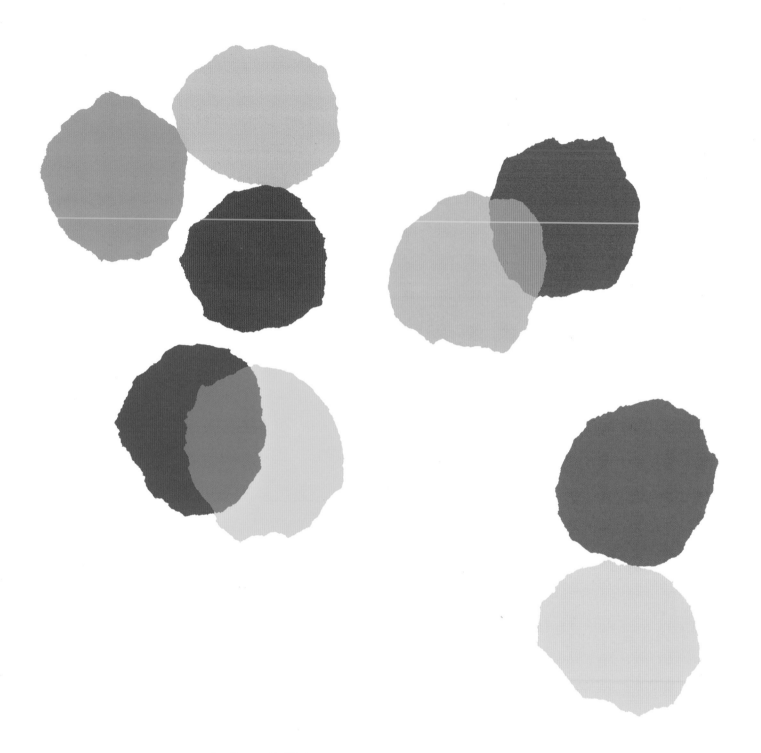

and the children played until suppertime.

The End

A NOTE TO PARENTS AND TEACHERS

Making a Book: *Little Blue and Little Yellow*

Leo Lionni tells how taking his two grandchildren, Pippo, age five, and Annie, age three, on the train from Grand Central Station in New York City to his home in Greenwich, Connecticut, resulted in his first children's book in 1959.

"They were an adorable pair, bright, lively, and totally uninhibited. It was the very first time I was alone with them, but they were intimidated enough by the surroundings and the uniqueness of the occasion to be on their best behavior.

"We were early and the car was almost empty, and in no time the two little angels had been transformed into two devilish little acrobats jumping from seat to seat. . . . Since more and more passengers were beginning to board the train, I realized that unless I did some fast creative thinking this was going to be one hell of a trip.

"I automatically opened my briefcase, took out an advance copy of Life, *and showed the children the cover, and tried to say something funny about the ads as I turned the pages, until a page with a design in blue, yellow, and green gave me an idea. 'Wait,' I said, 'I'll tell you a story.' I ripped the page out of the magazine and tore it into small pieces. The children followed the proceedings with intense expectancy. I took a piece of blue paper and carefully tore it into small disks. Then I did the same with pieces of yellow and green paper. I put my briefcase on my knees to make a table and in a deep voice said, 'This is Little Blue, and this is Little Yellow.'"*

Excerpt from *Between Worlds: The Autobiography of Leo Lionni*